Acknowledgments:
Models made by Whoopee! Productions Limited
Backgrounds illustrated by John Dillow. Layout designed by Liz Antill

British Library Cataloguing in Publication Data

Hately, David
　　Rupert and the paper mystery.
　　I. Title　　II. Bestall, Alfred　　III. Series
　　823′.914 [J]
　　ISBN 0-7214-1342-0

First edition

Published by Ladybird Books Ltd Loughborough Leicestershire UK
Ladybird Books Inc Auburn Maine 04210 USA

Printed in England (3)

RUPERT
and the
Paper Mystery

Based on the original story *Rupert and the Paper-fall*
by Alfred Bestall MBE
Adapted by David Hately

Ladybird Books

One cold afternoon, Rupert Bear went for a country walk. As he strolled along, he thought about Christmas and wondered what presents Santa might bring.

Suddenly, something white came floating down in front of his nose. He looked up and was surprised to see a shower of paper falling from the sky.

Rupert picked up the sheets of paper and took them home to show his daddy.

"These are lists of names and addresses in nearby villages," Mr Bear explained. "They don't mention Nutwood, though."

But Mr Bear couldn't tell who owned the papers.

"It's a mystery!" he said.

The next day was Christmas Eve.
Rupert was woken early by a noise
in the garden. He ran to the window to
see what was happening outside.

To his surprise, he saw a
sheet of paper lying by
the garden gate.

"That wasn't there
yesterday!" he
exclaimed.

Rupert dressed as quickly as he could. He ran outside and picked up the sheet of paper.

On it was a list of names and addresses, exactly like the others!

Rupert glanced down the lane and there, just disappearing round a bend, he saw a little old man.

Rupert dashed indoors to fetch all the papers he had collected. Then he ran down the lane and soon caught up with the old man, who was also clutching a bundle of papers.

"Excuse me!" said Rupert. "Do these lists belong to you?"

When the little old man saw the papers, he tried to snatch them. "Give them to me!" he cried.

"**B**ut what are they?" asked Rupert. "And why did they fall out of the sky?"

"Don't ask so many questions!" snapped the little old man, whisking the papers from Rupert's hand. Then, in a flash, he dodged past the little bear and took to his heels.

Puzzled, Rupert decided to follow the old man. He trotted after him until he reached a lake.

And there he saw another little man.

This one was dressed in overalls like an engineer. He was holding a long stick and trying to fish something out of the water.

"Can I help?" asked Rupert.

The engineer jumped when Rupert spoke. "Bother!" he said. "No one is supposed to see me! But I could do with your help."

Together they pulled a big, shiny toy car out of the lake.

"I was testing it," said the engineer, "and it went straight into the water! I've got to mend the steering wheel."

The engineer soon mended the steering wheel and climbed into the driving seat. Rupert said, "It's a lovely car! Just what I want for Christmas!"

The engineer stared at Rupert. "What's your name?" he asked. "And where do you live?"

"I'm Rupert Bear from Nutwood."

"Rupert Bear. Nutwood," repeated the engineer two or three times. Then he drove away.

Next morning, Rupert woke up and yawned. Suddenly he remembered what day it was!

"Christmas Day!" he shouted joyfully.

He climbed out of bed and there, right beside him, was his Christmas present.

It was the shiny car that he'd helped to pull from the lake!

After breakfast, Rupert pedalled his
new car down the lane to meet his
friends. But they were all
very gloomy. Santa had
sent them nothing at all!
Rupert was the only one
in Nutwood with a
Christmas present.

"It's a mystery!"
said Rupert, and he
began to tell them
about the fall of
papers from
the sky.

"**I** found a sheet of paper, too!" cried Bill Badger, pulling it from his pocket. "It has Nutwood names and addresses on it."

Rupert decided to investigate.

"You can all play with my car," he said. "I'm going to look for the little engineer."

Edward Trunk was too big and heavy to play with the toy car, so he decided to go with Rupert.

The pals went to the lake and began to follow the tracks left by the toy car.

But the tracks came to a sudden stop by a big rock.

N ear the rock they saw yet another little man. He was dressed as a jester, and he was hunting for something in the grass.

"Is this what you're looking for?" asked Rupert, holding up the paper that Bill had found. "It's a list of Nutwood names!"

The jester tried to snatch the paper, but Rupert held it out of reach. "We want to know what this is all about!" he said.

"I haven't time to explain!" answered the little jester. "You'd better come and see for yourselves."

He told Rupert and Edward Trunk to stand by the big rock and turn round three times from left to right.

On the third turn they felt a tingling feeling and, when they looked up, they were standing outside a building that had magically appeared out of nowhere!

"You must wait outside," the jester said to Edward Trunk. "Only the bear can come in."

Once inside the building, the jester darted off along a corridor. Rupert looked around him.

He was in a warehouse full of exciting parcels of all shapes and sizes. Little workmen were busily sorting them out into piles.

But although Rupert was indoors, stars and sparks kept shooting past his head!

When the jester returned, he brought with him the little old man who had snatched Rupert's papers. "Give me the Nutwood addresses, please!" the old man said.

"Not until you tell me where I am!" replied Rupert.

So the old man began to explain.

"**T**his is one of Santa's district warehouses," said the old man.

"We handle all presents for the Nutwood area.

"Unfortunately, a moon rocket flew too close to Santa's castle in the sky. It blew all the instructions for this district off his desk. They landed on earth and we searched everywhere for them. You found most of the papers. Only the Nutwood list was missing. That's why your friends didn't get any Christmas presents!"

Rupert offered to help to sort out the Nutwood presents, and the jester and the engineer loaded them all onto a sledge.

"**T**he sledge is a present for Algy Pug," the old man said, "but there isn't time to wrap it."

Outside the warehouse, Rupert and Edward Trunk held tightly to the sledge and turned round three times. But this time they turned from right to left and, once more, they found themselves standing by the big rock.

They dragged the sledge to Nutwood, where their eager pals gathered round to listen to Rupert's story.

Everyone had a parcel except Algy Pug. "Nothing for me!" he said sadly.

"Don't worry!" answered Rupert. "The sledge is for you!"

"It's just what I wanted!" said Algy, his eyes shining.

Algy asked Rupert to take him to the big rock and they pedalled there in Rupert's car.

"Did you really get into Santa's warehouse just by turning round?" Algy asked.

Rupert nodded, and the pug began spinning round and round until he was dizzy.

But the magic had gone!

"Perhaps it only works when one of Santa's helpers is nearby," said Rupert.

Rupert pedalled home, where his daddy was waiting for him by the gate.

"Hello!" the little bear called out. "That paper shower started such an adventure!"

Mr Bear smiled. "Come on," he said, "let's go inside and you can tell me all about it."